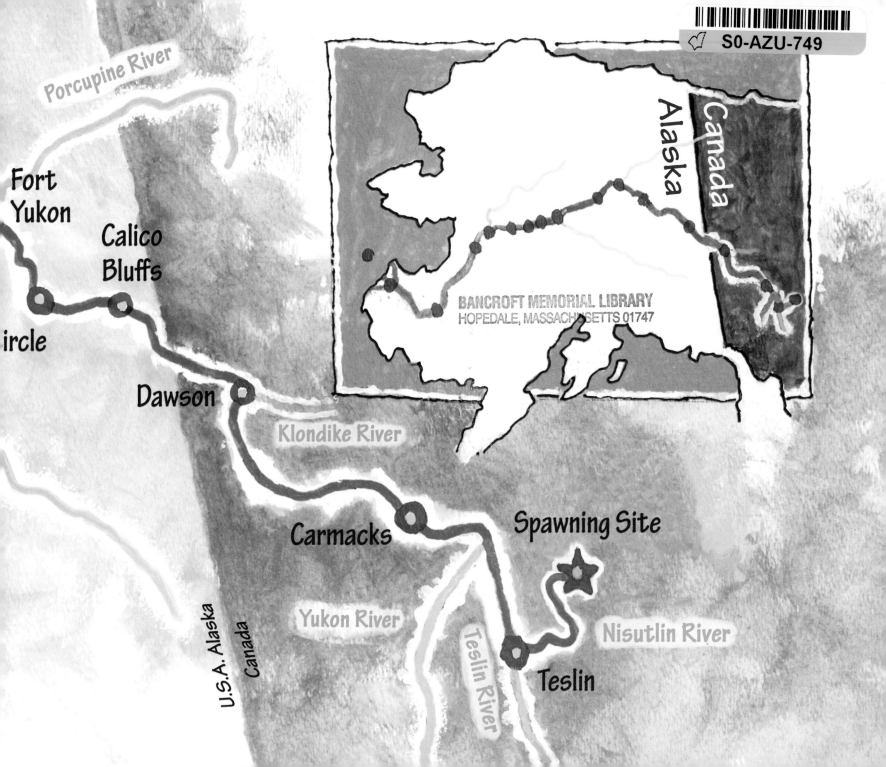

Porcupine River

Fort
Yukon

Calico
Bluffs

ircle

Dawson

Klondike River

Carmacks

Spawning Site

Yukon River

Nisutlin River

U.S.A. Alaska

Canada

Teslin River

Teslin

Alaska

Canada

For Noah

Enjoy following this salmon up the Yukon

♡

Debbie S. Miller

A King Salmon Journey

Debbie S. Miller *and* John H. Eiler
illustrated by Jon Van Zyle

University of Alaska Press
Fairbanks, Alaska

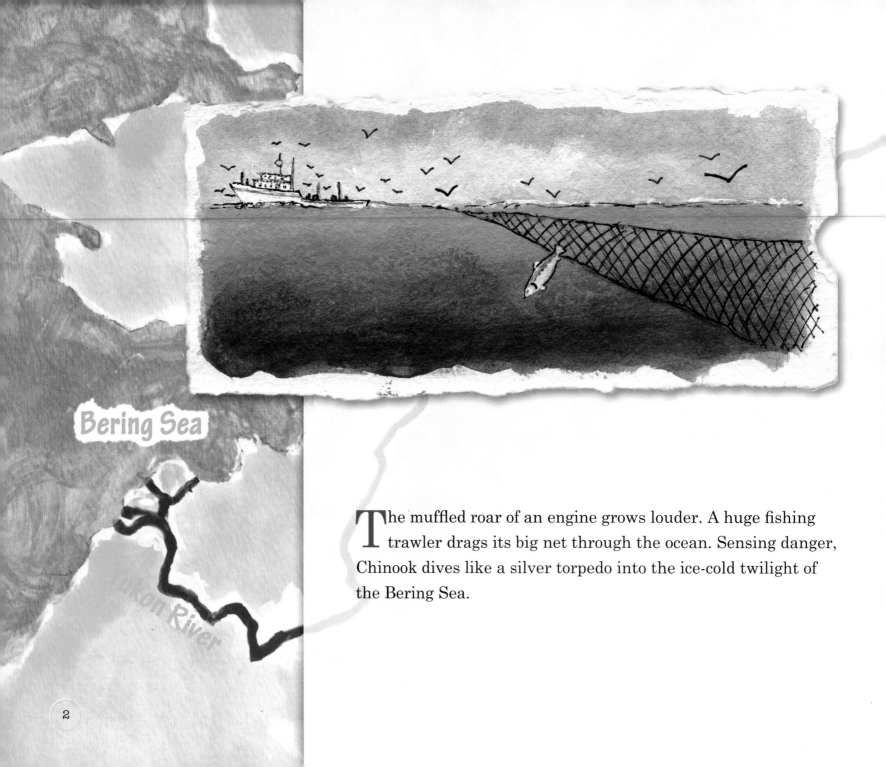

Bering Sea

Yukon River

The muffled roar of an engine grows louder. A huge fishing trawler drags its big net through the ocean. Sensing danger, Chinook dives like a silver torpedo into the ice-cold twilight of the Bering Sea.

A six-year-old king salmon, Chinook glides beneath a large school of pollock. She adjusts to the changing water pressure by releasing air bubbles from her swim bladder through her mouth. Descending more than 1,000 feet into the deep darkness, she uses her excellent vision to spot a sparkly creature with hooked arms and wing-like fins. With a powerful flick of her tail, Chinook rockets through the water and snatches a bioluminescent squid, one of her favorite meals.

Bering Sea

Yukon River

Chinook has a streamlined body covered with small, delicate scales. Her silvery skin has a slick coating that allows her to move easily through the water. For the past four years she has traveled across the open sea, feeding on a buffet of foods that include tiny zooplankton, shrimp-like krill, small fish, and squid.

This diet helped her grow from a finger-sized smolt to a 30-pound salmon rich with oils that give her energy to swim, catch food, and escape from predators.

Squeak . . . chirp . . . click. The strange voices sound like a blend of creaking doors and chirping birds. A pod of beluga whales chase a school of herring. Their white bodies look like ghosts flying underwater. These whales also eat salmon, but Chinook's dark back and light belly create countershading. This combination of colors provides excellent camouflage from predators looking down into the dark water or up into the sunlit water. After the pod leaves, Chinook catches a wiggly herring while cormorants dive for fish in a frenzy of churning water.

Bering Sea

Yukon River

Chinook feels a powerful urge to return to the freshwater stream where she was born. Like most salmon, Chinook is an anadromous fish. These fish are born in freshwater then swim to saltwater where they spend most of their lives. When fully grown, they return to their birthplace to spawn. Chinook is ready to join one of the longest fish migrations in the world, but how will she find her way?

Salmon have a strong homing instinct and can navigate across the ocean to the rivers where they were born, but how they do this is a mystery! It's like they have a secret compass and map inside their brains. Salmon have tiny fragments of magnetite in their snouts, which may work like a compass to help them swim in the correct direction. Imagine having a compass in your head that told you which direction was north!

Salmon may also use the position of the sun, smell, temperature, and flow of water to guide them. As Chinook reaches the mouth of the Yukon River, she is joined by thousands of other salmon, all following invisible underwater highways.

ALAKANUK
Date: June 12
Day: 2
River mile: 10
Elevation: 0'
Fish's speed: Unknown
Fish's depth: Unknown
Water temp: Unknown

Bering Sea

Alakanuk

In the estuary, Chinook adjusts to the mixture of fresh and salt water. In the ocean she drank water constantly, and her gills pumped the excess salt from her bloodstream into the sea. Now her body works in reverse, and she drinks very little. Instead of flushing salt out her gills, she absorbs the tiny traces of salt in fresh water. This remarkable adaptation, known as osmoregulation, keeps the liquids in her body in balance.

The distinct smell of the Yukon River is familiar to Chinook. This is the long river that she simply floated down as a young smolt, carried along by the current. Now she must retrace the journey to her birthplace by swimming upriver against the mighty flow of North America's third largest river drainage.

Chinook enters the river near Flat Island, where the main channel is nearly a mile wide. She swims by Alakanuk (ah-LUCK-uh-nuck), a Yup'ik Eskimo village.

Here villagers are mending fish nets and
building drying racks for the salmon harvest.
It's a busy time of year for these people who
have depended on salmon for thousands of
years. School is out and children are excited to
play in the midnight sun as they wait for the
first salmon.

Chinook works her way up the river, adjusting
to the freshwater environment. She swims
by other Yup'ik villages and often hears
motorboats as many fishermen set their
driftnets to catch the salmon.

RUSSIAN MISSION
Date: June 18
Day: 8
River mile: 188
Elevation: 26'
Fish's speed: 38 miles/day
Fish's depth: 11-84'
Water temp: 59°F

Yukon River

Tagging Station at Russian Mission

After nearly a week she reaches Russian Mission, where the first Russian fur trading post was established in 1837. The Yup'ik Eskimos have a traditional name for their village: Iqurmiut, meaning "people of the point."

Chinook swims past Circle Island, which is shaped like a perfect half-circle. Suddenly, she feels soft mesh drifting across her face. The driftnet catches her, but gentle hands quickly remove her from the net and place her in a cradle of water. Two scientists carefully slide a small radio tag into her stomach. The tag won't bother her because salmon do not eat during the migration. This internal tag is better than an external one that might damage her skin or affect her swimming.

Chinook is gently released back into the river, and she continues her journey up the Yukon. The radio tag sends out signals that tell the scientists her location, swimming depth, and the water's temperature. The scientists have given Chinook a voice so that they can learn more about her.

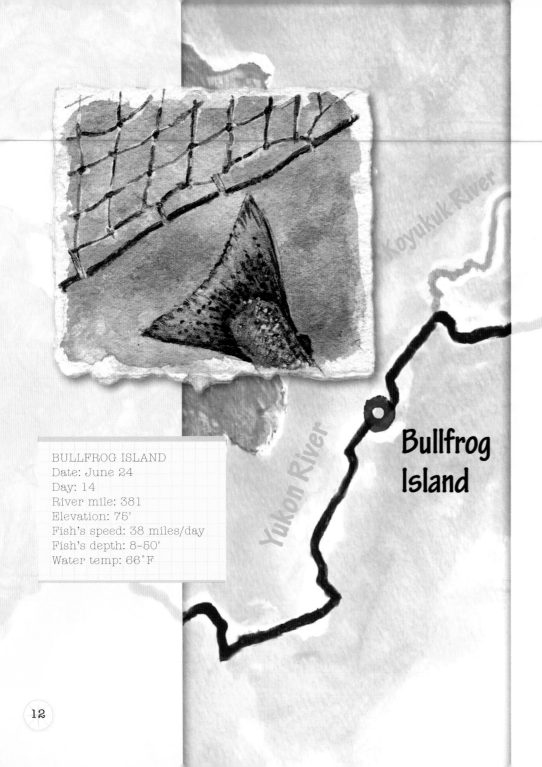

BULLFROG ISLAND
Date: June 24
Day: 14
River mile: 381
Elevation: 75'
Fish's speed: 38 miles/day
Fish's depth: 8-50'
Water temp: 66°F

Koyukuk River

Yukon River

Bullfrog Island

Chinook travels steadily at one to two miles per hour. Visibility is poor. The river is so clouded with powdery silt that it looks like a creamy cup of coffee. The tiny silt particles make a sizzling sound as they rub against each other in the water, like the fizzing sound of soda when poured in a glass.

Chinook moves along a deep, fast-moving stretch of river. Many fish are funneling through this narrow channel. Suddenly, she feels a pressure change from something in the water. She dives to the bottom and avoids the driftnet of a fisherman. The net brushes the tip of her dorsal fin, but she escapes. The fishing boat continues to drift downstream.

Chinook reaches a large, willow-fringed island known as Bullfrog Island.

She veers into a slow-moving slough where she can rest. Northern pintails and other ducks dabble on insects and vegetation in the shallow water next to her.

KOYUKUK
Date: June 27
Day: 17
River mile: 488
Elevation: 115'
Fish's speed: 38 miles/day
Fish's depth: 4-52'
Water temp: 62°F

Koyukuk River

Koyukuk

Many miles upriver from this quiet slough, a Koyukon Indian family gathers around the campfire at their fish camp. They've set their fishing net in an eddy along the Koyukuk River, a major tributary that flows into the Yukon.

"Grandma, can you tell us a riddle?" a grandchild asks.

Riddles and stories are usually told during the long winter nights, but Grandma thinks of a good one for summer.

"Wait, I see something: we come upstream in red canoes."

"People are coming to visit our camp?" the grandchild guesses.

"Think of something in the water," Grandma hints.

"Salmon!" the child claps.

While this family waits patiently for the fish to arrive, Chinook resumes her migration. Her silvery body is slowly changing to a bright reddish color. When she reaches the Koyukuk River, some salmon turn up this tributary, swimming to spawning sites farther upstream. A few of the fish are caught in the family's net, and Grandma shows her grandchildren how to untangle them from the mesh.

Chinook constantly smells the water through a pair of nares (rhymes with carries) on top of her snout. After she passes Galena, she detects a change in the water's chemistry. The Yukon's scent is stronger along the left bank, so she moves to the north side of the river. Other fish move toward the south bank, where they smell water from the Tanana River. The salmon's sense of smell can recognize two distinct currents more than 200 miles downstream.

Swish . . . Swish . . . Swish. Near Ruby, the churning paddles and baskets of a fish wheel rotate through the river like a Ferris wheel. Chinook avoids the area by swimming in deeper water.

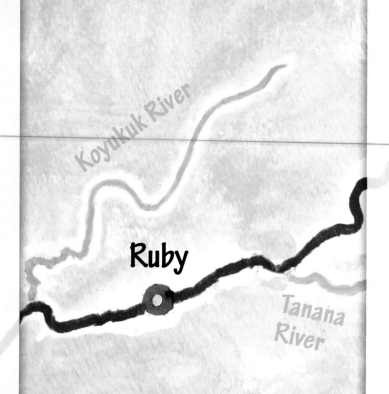

Koyukuk River

Ruby

Tanana River

RUBY
Date: June 29
Day: 19
River mile: 569
Elevation: 138'
Fish's speed: 37 miles/day
Fish's depth: 6-50'
Water temp: 70°F

The fish wheel's baskets scoop up chum salmon that swim in shallow water near the shore. They slide down a chute into a fish box.

On the riverbank, Florence Esmailka is cutting salmon on a table while her husband, Harold, removes salmon from the fish box. As he reaches down to pull out a fish, a big salmon slides down the chute and surprises him as it thumps into the box. Soon their drying racks and smokehouse will be filled with salmon, which they will eat all year.

Chinook has not eaten for three weeks, and her stomach looks like a deflated balloon. Yet her body's rich oil gives her plenty of energy for the migration. Swimming hundreds of miles against the strong current is tiring, so she chooses underwater pathways with less resistance. As she approaches a big bend, she follows the inside curve of the river where the current is weaker, avoiding the sweeping flow along the outer bank.

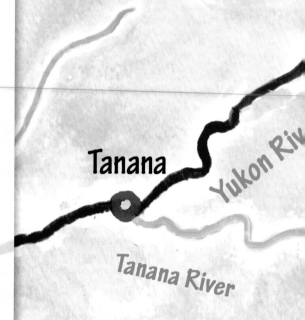

Tanana

Yukon Riv

Tanana River

TANANA
Date: July 1
Day: 21
River mile: 688
Elevation: 200'
Fish's speed: 43 miles/day
Fish's depth: 4-42'
Water temp: 67°F

The river is fringed with thick willows and black spruce. As Chinook swims around
Fox Island, a pair of trumpeter swans flies overhead. Arcing their graceful wings,
they fly toward the ponds within the Nowitna National Wildlife Refuge. Many swans,
ducks, and songbirds are nesting in the refuge. On the tip of the island, a huge bull
moose browses on the new leafy growth of the willows.

When she reaches Tanana, hundreds of thousands of salmon branch off and migrate
up the Tanana River. Chinook and many other salmon continue following the Yukon.

The river begins to narrow and Chinook swims faster. Steep faces of the Ray Mountains look over the river valley. At Rampart Rapids, the swift current pushes Chinook toward the riverbank. Suddenly, she is spinning through the air in a fish wheel basket: splash! Sliding down the wheel's chute, she falls back into the river. She has just been counted by students at the Rapids Research Center, a salmon monitoring site. Although she is startled by the ride, Chinook continues moving upriver.

Chinook passes Steven's Village on the Fourth of July. The river twists and turns as she enters the slow-moving waters of the Yukon Flats. Unlike Rampart Rapids, the river is braided with many channels, gravel bars, and sloughs. Sometimes Chinook has to search for the best route. She swims much slower as she works her way across this flat, sprawling wetlands.

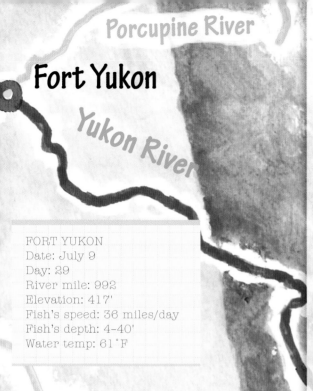

Porcupine River

Fort Yukon

Yukon River

FORT YUKON
Date: July 9
Day: 29
River mile: 992
Elevation: 417'
Fish's speed: 36 miles/day
Fish's depth: 4-40'
Water temp: 61°F

Following a shallow side channel, she feels her dorsal fin rising above the surface. She quickly turns around and wriggles back downstream to find a deeper channel. Soon she approaches the Gwich'in Indian community of Fort Yukon. Many people are at fish camps drying fish on racks along the Yukon, which means "big river" in the Gwich'in language.

Near Fort Yukon, Chinook feels a surge of water from another tributary, the Porcupine River. Although other king salmon return to this river to spawn, Chinook knows this tributary will not lead her home.

As Chinook continues to follow the Yukon, another female salmon turns up the Porcupine. This fish detours up the tributary for more than 200 miles before realizing she is in the wrong place. Turning around, she swims back to the Yukon and continues searching for her birthplace.

Chinook approaches the old gold rush town of Circle. Nearby, two wildfires are burning out of control. Waves of smoke drift along the Yukon, and black spruce trees along the shore look like flaming torches. Suddenly, Chinook senses splashing in the water. A cow moose and her two calves are thrashing across the river. Their hooves just miss hitting Chinook as they escape the raging fire.

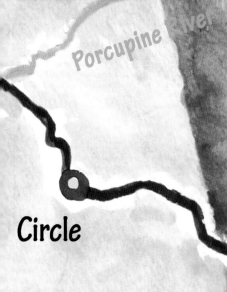

Porcupine River

Circle

CIRCLE
Date: July 12
Day: 32
River mile: 1096
Elevation: 600'
Fish's speed: 36 miles/day
Fish's depth: 4-27'
Water temp: 61°F

U.S.A. Alaska

Canada

Chinook is halfway home, but she still has more than 1,000 miles to go. Beyond the forest fires, she swims through a peaceful stretch of the Yukon. The silver surface of the river is slick and smooth as it slides through the wide, forested valley.

Rounding a big bend, Chinook passes Calico Bluff. This colorful wall of sedimentary rock layers is tilted and folded, like someone dropped an enormous layer cake on its side right next to the river. The beautiful bluff is located near an unstable fault zone, where the earth's layers have shifted and moved over time.

Chinook notices the shadows of cliff swallows as they dart above the surface of the Yukon, snatching mosquitoes. whwhwhWHWHWHWHOOOOOSH! Like a jet plane ripping through the sky, a peregrine falcon plummets to earth, wings tucked tightly against its body. The falcon just misses one of the swallows as it zigzags away. This peregrine hunts to feed its growing chicks in a nest perched on a cliff above the river.

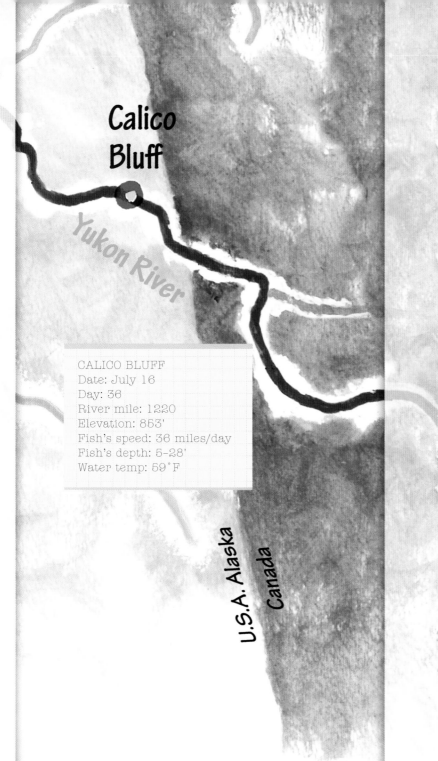

Calico Bluff

Yukon River

CALICO BLUFF
Date: July 16
Day: 36
River mile: 1220
Elevation: 853'
Fish's speed: 36 miles/day
Fish's depth: 5-28'
Water temp: 59°F

U.S.A. Alaska

Canada

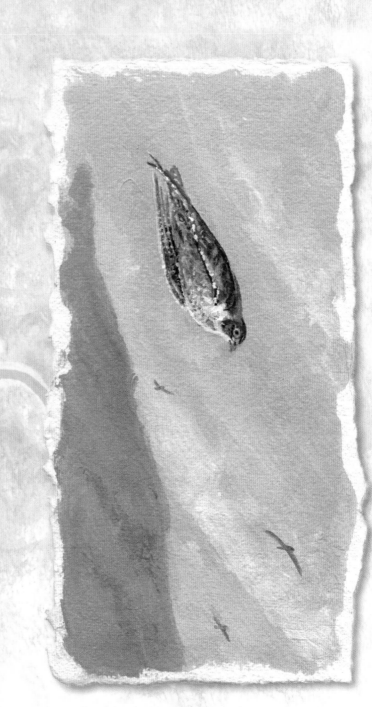

Chinook crosses into Canada and heads toward the historic gold rush town of Dawson. With warm summer days, the riverbanks and gravel bars explode with wildflowers.

Spoosh-ah-whoosh . . . spoosh-ah-whoosh . . . spoosh-ah-whoosh. Chinook senses turbulence in the water. She avoids a sternwheeler and its huge paddles as they churn through the river. During the first half of the twentieth century, many sternwheelers carried freight and passengers up and down the Yukon. Today, this boat only carries visitors who are learning about the region's history.

Chinook can smell the water of the Klondike, a tributary where gold was discovered in 1896. Like the prospectors who rushed up this river in search of gold, several salmon speed up this tributary to spawn. Klondike king salmon are among the fastest swimmers in the Yukon drainage, traveling more than 38 miles per day.

Chinook passes Tr'ochek, a summer fishing camp where Han Indians once traveled in birch bark canoes and scooped salmon out of the river using handmade nets.

DAWSON
Date: July 18
Day: 38
River mile: 1330
Elevation: 1047'
Fish's speed: 38 miles/day
Fish's depth: 3-44'
Water temp: 60°F

Dawson

After two more days of travel, Chinook feels a distinct change in pressure and current. She swims blindly and slowly through thick clouds of powdery silt that coat her gills as she struggles to breathe.

Chinook powers through the confluence of the Yukon and the White River. This huge tributary dumps millions of tons of silt into the Yukon. Each summer the immense glaciers of the Wrangell and St. Elias mountains move, carve, and grind the rock beneath them. The steady rush of melting ice causes tremendous erosion.

Suddenly the clouds of silt disappear as Chinook surges beyond the murky White River. The Yukon is clear! Chinook's keen eyes spot other fish in the river. Arctic grayling feed at the mouth of a creek. A northern pike lunges at a small whitefish, while a huge, black burbot lingers by a submerged log.

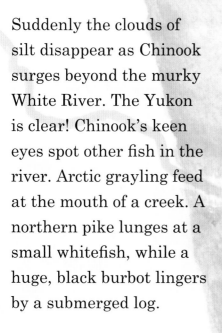

Carmacks

Yukon River

CARMACKS
Date: July 25
Day: 45
River mile: 1575
Elevation: 1739'
Fish's speed: 31 miles/day
Fish's depth: 3-19'
Water temp: 63°F

Finally Chinook detects the scent of the Teslin River. With a thrust of her tail, she leaves the Yukon behind. Five years ago, she lived in the sheltered pools and eddies of the Teslin, feeding on tiny insects and hiding from predatory fish in the shaded waters. Now, she spots young salmon parr feeding in a sheltered pool behind a log jam she once used.

Chinook is a different fish now. Her skin, once silvery, has turned dark red. She has lost a lot of weight during the migration, but she still has enough energy to continue.

She reaches a lake known to the Tlingit Indians as Tes-lin-Too, meaning "long, narrow water." As Chinook swims along the shore of this sparkling lake, she searches for her natal stream. She passes the village of Teslin and swims beneath a long bridge. Then she detects the trace minerals flowing from the Nisutlin River. The scent of her birthplace is more intense than ever.

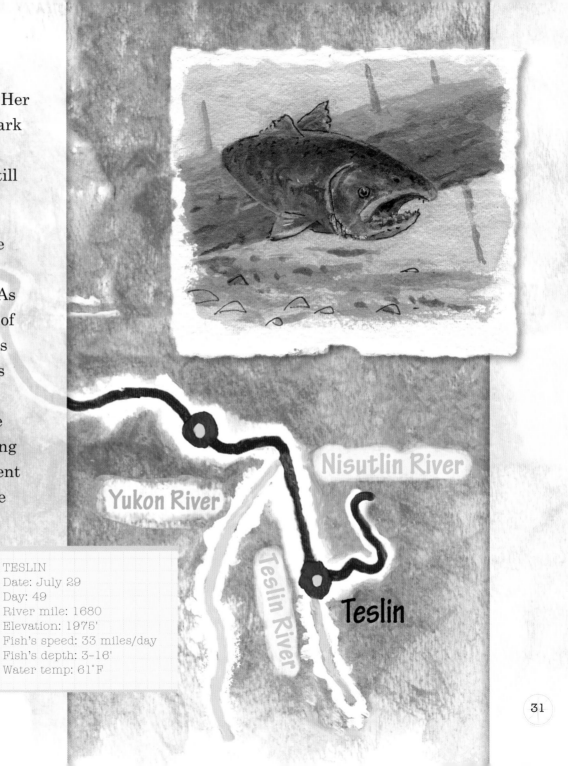

TESLIN
Date: July 29
Day: 49
River mile: 1680
Elevation: 1975'
Fish's speed: 33 miles/day
Fish's depth: 3–16'
Water temp: 61°F

Nisutlin River

Yukon River

Teslin River

Teslin

Chinook travels through water as clear as glass with the spruce forest casting an emerald glow through the water. Her surroundings have dramatically changed from the creamy brown swirl of the deep and wide Yukon, to the crystal-clear riffles and pools of the narrow and shallow Nisutlin. She is almost home.

Wolf, beaver, and bear tracks line the sandbars as Chinook makes her way up the Nisutlin. She finds a coarse gravel patch in the streambed near the place where she emerged from an egg six years ago. Coming back to the same place helps to ensure that her own eggs will develop successfully. After swimming 2,007 miles, Chinook is home.

In the clear, cool (55°F) water she claims her nesting place, known as a redd. She chases away other female salmon that wander by. Several feet below the surface, she turns on her side, arches her back, and fans the gravel with her tail. She gradually creates a foot-deep pocket where she will deposit her eggs. The good current means the eggs will have oxygen-rich water for healthy development. As she digs, a grizzly bear prowls for salmon along the riverbank.

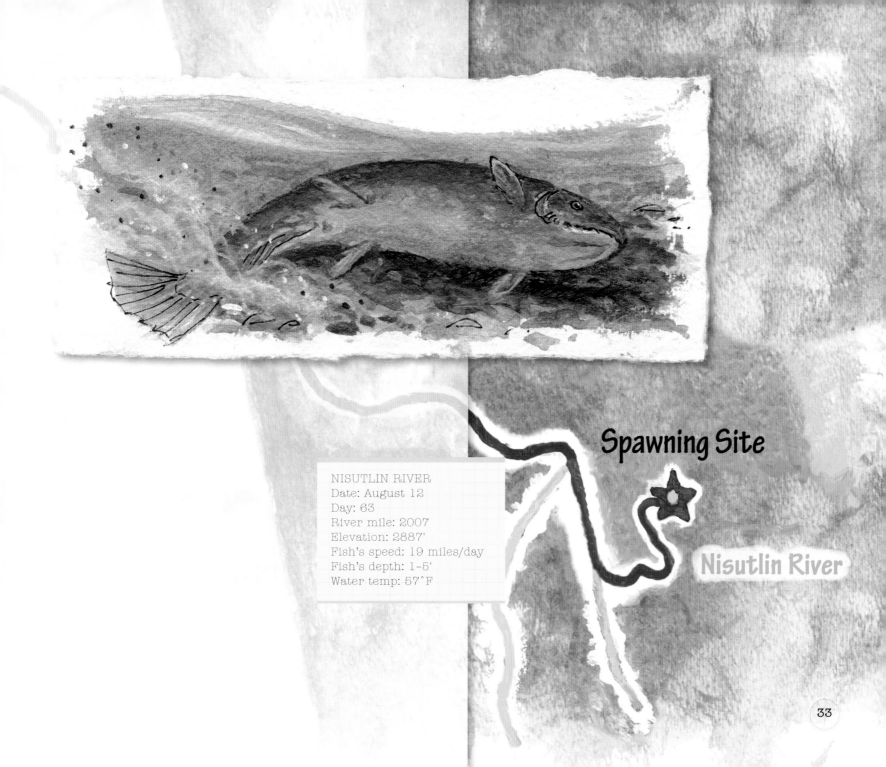

NISUTLIN RIVER
Date: August 12
Day: 63
River mile: 2007
Elevation: 2887'
Fish's speed: 19 miles/day
Fish's depth: 1-5'
Water temp: 57°F

Spawning Site

Nisutlin River

While she prepares her redd, a large male salmon with a hooked snout, or kype, joins her. He chases away other males that want to be Chinook's mate. He guards the redd, constantly swimming back and forth around Chinook. He often swims beside her, quivering his body as part of the mating ritual.

Splash! The huge paws of the grizzly bear thrash through the water near the shore. This powerful predator snatches a smaller male salmon in the shallows. Chinook and her mate are safe because their redd is in deeper water.

The hungry grizzly carries the salmon into the woods and consumes most of it. The leftovers will provide food for bald eagles and ravens, wolves and foxes, and many smaller creatures. The nutrients from the carcass will also fertilize the trees and plants along the river. This forest is healthy and vibrant because of the salmon.

NISUTLIN RIVER
Date: August 17
Day: 68
River mile: 2007
Elevation: 2887'
Fish's speed: 0 miles/day
Fish's depth: 1-5'
Water temp: 57°F

Spawning Site

Nisutlin River

When Chinook is ready, she drops her belly into the redd and opens her mouth wide. The male swims at her side, his black-rimmed mouth also gaping. It is as though they are saying "I'm ready!" Chinook squeezes out some of the eggs, and her mate instantly releases a white cloud of milt. Once the eggs leave Chinook's body they must be fertilized within twenty seconds, or they will not develop.

After the eggs sink into the redd, Chinook carefully buries them, fanning gravel into the pocket with her tail. She digs several more pockets so that all of her 10,000 eggs can be deposited. Releasing eggs in different locations gives a better chance for some of them to survive.

Chinook guards the redd and its precious treasure. While she hovers over the hidden eggs, a brilliant moon rises above the forest and a wolf howls on the riverbank near her.

After protecting the nest for a week, Chinook is exhausted. She no longer has the strength to swim against the current. On a crisp, autumn morning, Chinook floats downstream and dies. Her remains will feed algae and many tiny creatures that will become food for young salmon fry.

Next spring, Chinook's eggs will hatch and a
new generation of salmon will begin their lives.

We wish to thank the many people who helped with this project, including biologists from the Alaska Department of Fish and Game and the local individuals who shared their stories about salmon and life on the Yukon River. We also thank Dr. Katherine Myers and Dr. Thomas Quinn for their insights on salmon biology and life history.

For Mary Clare, thanks for following the salmon with me along the Yukon,

and

For Nels, my canoe partner, who shared a wonderful salmon journey down the Nisutlin River.

Cheers to these amazing swimmers!

—Debbie S. Miller

To Nancy, the love of my life, and my sons, Weston and Luke, who kept the home fires burning during my many years on the river.

—John H. Eiler

A story of nature's wildlife perseverance . . . Lessons to be learned by the human race.

—Jon Van Zyle

University of Alaska Press
P.O. Box 756240
Fairbanks, AK 99775-6240

Library of Congress Cataloging-in-Publication Data

Miller, Debbie S., 1951– author.
 A king salmon journey / by Debbie S. Miller and John H. Eiler ; illustrated by Jon Van Zyle.
    pages cm
 Audience: K to grade 3.
 ISBN 978-1-60223-230-3 (hardcover : alk. paper) — ISBN 978-1-60223-231-0 (paperback : alk. paper)
 1. Chinook salmon—Migration—Alaska—Juvenile literature. 2. Chinook salmon—Life cycles—Alaska—
Juvenile literature. I. Eiler, John H. (John Heinrich), 1953– author. II. Van Zyle, Jon, illustrator. III. Title.
 QL638.S2M478 2014
 597.5'6156—dc23

                        2013048828

Cover and text design by Paula Elmes, ImageCraft Publications & Design, and Jon Van Zyle.
Illustrations by Jon Van Zyle.

This publication was printed on acid-free paper that meets the minimum requirements for ANSI / NISO
Z39.48–1992 (R2002) (Permanence of Paper for Printed Library Materials).

Printed in China

SNOWY OWL BOOKS
an imprint of the University of Alaska Press

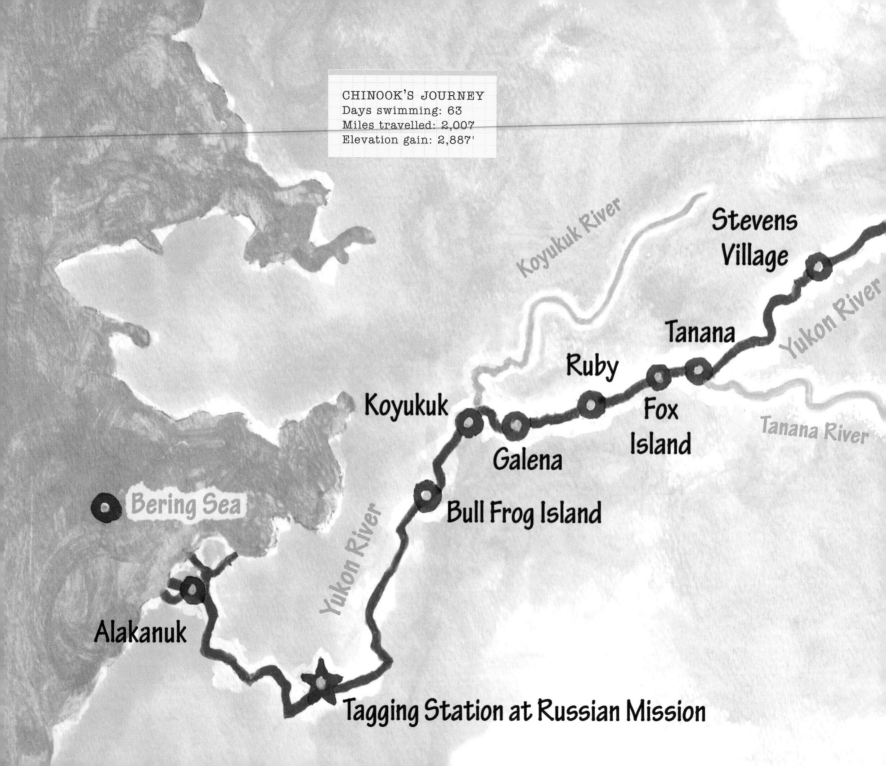

CHINOOK'S JOURNEY
Days swimming: 63
Miles travelled: 2,007
Elevation gain: 2,887'

Koyukuk River

Stevens
Village

Tanana

Ruby

Yukon River

Koyukuk

Fox
Island

Tanana River

Galena

Bering Sea

Bull Frog Island

Yukon River

Alakanuk

Tagging Station at Russian Mission